THE INCIDENT AT
OUTPOST 31

JOHN MERCIER

Cover concept by
John Mercier

Cover art by
Frederick Foss

Editing by
Red to Black Editing

Special Thanks

David Cordero
Kim Murphy
Wess Murphy
Brandie Heighes
Tina Chen

Chapter 1

For Robert, the opportunity to be the administrator of a deep space outpost seemed to be the chance of a lifetime, even though it wasn't considered a prestigious assignment. In fact, there was so little interest in the position, that the only way they could find anyone willing to fill it was to compensate with a higher than average salary.

He was only twenty-six, quite young to be employed in such a capacity—they usually only entrusted it to those with more experience. Robert had just graduated with his degree in technology management, with minors in robotics and computer sciences. He was more than qualified for this job, despite some reservations from the board of directors. Luckily for him, his instructors had recommended him highly, which assuaged the board's concerns.

GeoCorp was the world leader in Astrogeology and deep space mining, not to mention a multi-billion-credit company. Despite being overjoyed at the opportunity to work for such an established reputable employer, being in charge of a facility in the middle of nowhere, orbiting an uninhabited planet for a year wasn't exactly his dream job. It would, however, look great on his resume. It was all part of his plan to catapult himself out of the entry-level trenches and into a higher position in the company.

He had never been in charge of anything or anyone before, and this had him slightly worried. Miners weren't typically known as a polite, authority-respecting bunch, and he wondered if they would even listen to someone as young as he was. Not that he would really blame them, though; they had a dangerous job and got far less pay than they deserved, given the risk. He tried to calm these concerns by reassuring himself that the outposts were merely transfer and refueling stations, and that when they did show up, they would be gone in a day or two.

For the first couple months, everything went fine. He went about his daily routine, making his rounds and checking systems. The station pretty much ran itself; he only had to run his diagnostics twice a shift. In between, he wandered the station or visited the library, often wondering why they needed a human being out here at all. He supposed it was just a formality. The idea of letting some multi-million-credit facility out in the middle of nowhere run totally on automation without someone to keep an eye on things probably didn't sit well with the investors. And what could possibly happen?

He hadn't seen another human being since he stepped off the ship that brought him to the station. At first, the solitude was welcome. On Earth, everything was always so congested and suffocating; there always seemed to be someone over your shoulder. Sometimes, he'd get so sick of being around people that he felt like he couldn't breathe. Feeling claustrophobic, he'd close his eyes, count to ten, and imagine himself in some wide open space where you could spread your arms out as far they would go and not touch another person. Though here, alone all day with no one to talk to, week after week, month after month, he began to miss the clamor of other people.

One day, sitting at his console, he glanced over and noticed that the robot working at the control panel to his left seemed to be on the same schedule as he. The robots were basically humanoid in shape—except for their heads, which were more like horizontally mounted cylinders with a single large red optical eye and two smaller sensors that looked like nothing more than black dots. Their chassis were a dull, brushed aluminum, nothing fancy or ornate, just practical. He squinted to read the number on its chest plate.

"Number seventeen, huh? That's a boring name," he said. "How about I call you Charlie?"

Every day from that point on, he'd say hello to Charlie as if he were a colleague. He enjoyed the ruse. It made him laugh and alleviated the monotony of station life. One Friday, he even put a Hawaiian shirt on the robot and joked that it was casual Friday. But as the months rolled on, even Charlie's companionship started to lose its amusement.

This day started like all other days had started for the past four months. He begrudgingly plopped down into his chair at his console. He slouched over his panel and stared blankly at the monitor, like a zombie, and typed. He looked over to his left, and for the first time since he'd been on the station, the robot working there was not Charlie. He sat up in bewilderment. He got up from his chair and walked around the room, inspecting all the robots one by one, checking their numbers. None of them were Charlie.

"That's odd," he said. He went back to his console and sat down to finish initializing the diagnostic protocols. While he pondered Charlie's absence, a thought popped into his mind: *coffee*; and suddenly he craved it. He decided to put the great Charlie mystery on hold.

He got up and started down the corridor toward the cafeteria. About halfway there, he came across a service robot standing in the hallway, which was strange—there was no reason for a robot to ever stop in the corridors. As he got closer, he was able to make out its number: seventeen.

"Charlie!" he said. "What in the world are you doing out here?" The robot stood completely still, as if frozen in place—except for the jerking and twitching of its cylindrical head. It reminded him of the Tin Man from *Wizard of Oz*. Robert examined the catatonic machine. The small LED strip on its back blinked yellow.

"Standby mode?" he said aloud to himself. Typically the robots only entered standby mode while they were at the charging port. He patted the robot reassuringly on the shoulder.

"Don't worry, Charlie, after I get my coffee I'll get you fixed right up. Don't you go running off, now," he said, pointing at him with his index finger and thumb in mock portrayal of a gun.

Robert continued on his way to the cafeteria, somewhat relieved to have solved the riddle of where Charlie had gone. He walked into the cafeteria and the motion sensor activated the lights, which blinked momentarily before staying on. He went over to the coffee dispenser and filled a cup. He closed his eyes and inhaled, allowing the bitter aroma to sink deep into his olfactory senses before taking a sip. He looked around at the empty chairs and tables. It was like he was the last person in the universe, but at least he had all the comforts one could wish for. While standing there enjoying his coffee, he started to wonder how Charlie could have entered standby mode in the middle of a corridor; it gnawed at his curiosity.

He went back to the control room, sat down at his terminal, put his coffee down, and pulled up the automation display. There were forty-five robots on this station: thirty service robots and fifteen maintenance robots. Each one had its own icon and profile. You could click on an individual robot and it would list everything about it. Where it was, its serial number, charge level, what task it was running, bug reports, and they were color-coded depending on status: green for operational, yellow for standby mode, and red for malfunctioning. He pulled up the overview, which showed small thumbnails of all the robots on one screen, located number seventeen, and hit the button for manual reboot. He then directed Charlie to report to maintenance so he could take a closer look and run a full diagnostic on him.

By the time Robert got to maintenance, Charlie was already there waiting for him. Robert was confident he could get to the bottom of the issue, whatever it was. He sat down on his stool with his electric screwdriver in hand and unscrewed the bolts to the diagnostic panel, exposing a row of cable ports. He connected the robot to the diagnostic computer with a long, black cable.

"Let's see what's wrong with you," he said. He leaned over the console to his right and initiated the program.

After an hour of scans and physical examinations, everything came back normal. Because he couldn't find anything wrong, he began to speculate possible scenarios—perhaps some sort of electronic or magnetic interference from the nearby planet, or some unknown computer virus that the scans just weren't picking up.

Either way, instead of easing his concern, it made him start to feel more worried.

The next day started as they always did. He had never really noticed before, but now, as he made his rounds, there always seemed to be a robot everywhere he went, like they were keeping tabs on him; spying on him. Had they always been there? He stretched his memory, but couldn't remember. He had never really paid them much attention before. He wondered if maybe the mainframe itself had some glitch. That would explain things, since the robots were basically mindless automatons.

He decided to run a thorough scan of the mainframe. He wasn't sure exactly what he was looking for, but he hoped he might just stumble across something. While the scans analyzed the various programs, Robert leaned back in his chair and held his hand to his face, pressing his fingers against his forehead.

I hope this finds something, otherwise I'm out of ideas, he thought. He glanced over to check on the progress of the scan. It was only at twelve percent, so he decided to let it run and to check on it the next morning.

Even though he was alone on the station, he decided to lock the door to his sleeping quarters, though he felt a little ridiculous doing so. These silent sentinels of the station didn't even seem to acknowledge his presence, yet he locked himself in anyway. Being the only human on the station had started to make him anxious. He realized that, if the robots had somehow been compromised, there was no one to help him, and rescue was light years away. He lay awake in his bed, staring at the ceiling, wondering what to do next. Was there something wrong with the robots? If something was going on, did the machines know that he suspected an issue? What would they do if they did? These questions spiraled around his head, haunting him.

He awoke from his sleep cycle, showered, and dressed. He decided that it was best to continue about his daily routine while he tried to crack this enigma, so as not to alert them to his awareness. He walked to the door of his sleeping quarters and hesitantly clicked the green unlock button, swallowing hard. There was a metal clank as the lock released and the hum of electric actuators as door slid open. His heart pounded, his palms sweated, and his breathing got heavier.

You're being stupid, he thought. He summoned all the courage he could muster, stepped out into the hallway, and began his walk to the control room. He walked stiffly and swiftly, occasionally wiping sweat from his forehead with his sleeve. He had an eerie feeling that someone was staring at him from behind, but he dared not turn around to check.

He approached a maintenance robot heading the opposite way down the corridor. He felt his muscles tense, his heart pound, and his body flush hot as adrenaline streamed into his veins. Visions of the robot lunging at him danced through his imagination—but the machine simply walked by. Robert realized that he had been holding his breath, and let it expel from his lungs. He paused for a moment, turned to watch the robot until it went around the bend of the corridor and out of sight, and then he continued on to the control room.

Robert sat down in the chair at his station, his eyes locked on his console. The scan had run its course and had found no anomalies. He stared at the monitor in disbelief. All around the control room, the robots continued to work diligently. He could hear the metallic taps of their feet and the low whirring of their servos. He thought he could feel them watching him. For a moment, he was a child again, thinking that if he didn't look under his bed, the monster wouldn't be there.

He quickly started the daily diagnostic scans of the facility to keep up the façade. The diagnostics would run through programs systematically looking for required repairs. Life support, gravity generator, medical bay, fueling station, communications, robot maintenance, and lab operations. While the computer compiled data, he leaned over and checked the communications terminal. There was never anything there, but he had never hoped so much to see an incoming docking request from a ship, because at least then he wouldn't be alone. His heart sank, just as his body sank back into his chair. There were no boarding requests in queue. He let his eyes scan the control room, trying not to move his head. There were five service robots monitoring a multitude of subsystems, carrying out whatever the mainframe had directed them to do. He realized his life was truly in the hands of these machines.

That night, as Robert walked toward his sleeping quarters, he stopped and stared at a fire axe mounted on the wall. Firearms were restricted on the facility. There was too great a risk of puncturing the hull, despite the fact that the station was built so that sections could independently seal off in case of hull breach. He studied the axe for a moment as if it were a piece of art in a museum, then he took it off the wall, glanced around guiltily, and continued on to his quarters.

Robert shut and locked the security door behind him. He walked over and leaned the axe against the small table right beside his bed, then began stripping off his uniform. He set his boots on the floor next to his bed, dimmed the lights, and crawled under the covers. Sleep seemed to elude him. His brain was swimming in questions and fear poisoned his imagination. Every noise startled him, and his eyes would shoot wide open, the darkness of the room playing tricks on him. Regardless of all the distractions, he eventually drifted off to sleep.

Robert's eyes popped open instantaneously to the blaring, raucous station alarm. He rushed to get out of bed, but his legs were tangled in his sheets, causing him to trip and knock over the little table and the axe. He was on all fours on the floor, in the dark, feeling for his boots. The red warning lights began flashing, giving slight glimpses of sight in the otherwise darkened room. Finally, the small emergency backup lights came on, giving off just barely enough light to see.

What the hell is going on? he thought. In a panic, he rushed to throw on his uniform as fast as possible, squeezing his feet awkwardly into his boots, his hands shaking. He grabbed the axe and walked toward the door. He couldn't help but think that perhaps the robots were responsible for whatever was going on.

The door was electronically disabled, but Robert quickly pulled the manual override release lever. The door opened a mere crack. He stuck his fingers in the opening, grunting as he strained to pry it apart enough to fit through. The corridor was pitch black, except for the occasional strobe of red emergency guide lights on the floor. He cautiously made his way to the control room. Upon entering, he jetted down the few steps to where his console sat in the center of the room. The controls were blinking rhythmically, like lights on a Christmas tree. He punched the keys as fast as his fingers would go, as he tried to figure out what was happening.

Most of the station systems were down, or malfunctioning; and the console was not responding—it was completely useless. All the external sensors were completely offline, and the outer shield doors had closed; he was blind. He knew what he had to do, though he feared doing it.

The engineers had purposely put the mainframe down in the core of the station to give it the as much shielding as possible from any sort of electromagnetic pulse The only chance he had to get the station back online was to go down through the maintenance hatch to the core of the station and manually reset the relays to reboot the system. That meant going down in the dark, alone, in a small confined space, the perfect setup for an ambush.

What if this is an elaborate plan? A trap set by the robots? he wondered. But, doing nothing wasn't an option. The life support and emergency systems would only last so long.

Realizing he had no choice, he walked over to the maintenance hatch on the floor behind his console. He knelt down and slid his key into the lock, which popped up a small, silver, T-shaped handle that was embedded flush with the hatch. He twisted it ninety degrees, pulled it down, and the hatch opened with a clunk. When he pried the hatch open, he was met with a pillar of hot air that emanated from the darkness and punched him in the face. He removed a small flashlight from his belt and shined it down the hole and saw nothing but the grated floor down below. He grabbed his axe and slowly descended the tiny metal rungs protruding from the wall.

When he hit the bottom, he shined his light in both directions, expecting to find something lurking there in the shadows, but there was nothing. The heat was unbearable. Beads of sweat formed on his brow and around his nose. His uniform clung tightly to his body. He had to slightly crouch down as he walked through the tunnel, which was not much larger than a crawlspace. He doubted he would even have room to swing the axe if he needed to, but he felt better having it anyway.

The dark, cramped tunnel finally gave way to a slightly larger circular room where he could at least stand upright: He had reached the core. The core was housed in a large room, but the walkway was a small, ring-shaped catwalk encircling the anti-matter engine that powered the station. All kinds of large hoses, wires, and pipes ran from all directions overhead and attached to the center engine. He shined his light at the walls and started his search for the breaker relays.

As he walked around the ring, his footsteps on the metal grating clanked and echoed in the enormous room. The humidity made the air thick and hard to breath. He reached the relay center, and felt a little better. He had temporarily forgotten about the robots, totally focused as he was on the relays, which had all been tripped. One by one, he reached out to the red handles and reset them to the up position with a loud snap. Underneath the red handles, green buttons started to light up, indicating that the circuits were ready to be closed. He quickly clicked them as fast as he could. Now, with the relays reset, he needed to find the mainframe console to initiate a hard reboot.

He scurried along the dark catwalk until he found it. He stuck his key into the keyhole on the console and turned it. He opened the panel to reveal the palm scanner and keypad. He wiped his hand on his uniform to dry off the sweat, and then placed it on the scanner. It lit up greenish-blue in an oscillating wave under his hand. The display screen read: "ENTER SECURITY CODE." He touched the screen to enter his clearance code, which beeped on every digit. The screen changed to read: "AUTHORIZED," then switched to a menu display. He quickly perused the options until he saw what he was looking for: "REBOOT SYSTEM." He pressed it with a sigh of relief. The lights remained off, but he knew it was only a matter of time before they came on, so he started back toward the ladder.

He made it as far as the relay center when he stopped dead in his tracks in response to the most terrifying sound he could imagine: metal footsteps in the abyss, echoing throughout the core room. All of the maintenance tunnels led from different parts of the station and ran to the central core, but it was almost impossible to distinguish which direction the footsteps were coming from. He shined his light feverishly in all directions.

They must have realized I rebooted the system, he thought. He gripped the axe tightly in his hand as his mind and heart raced.

He needed to get out of the core as soon as possible, and decided to quietly make his way back toward the tunnel that led to the control room. He truly dreaded the thought of the maintenance tunnel. In there, in the dark, he would be helpless, and it was a relatively long distance to the ladder. He got to the entrance of the tunnel, stopped, and strained his ears to listen. The footsteps were getting louder. His mouth ran dry and fear ran wild through his body. He knew almost instantly there would be no sneaking past his mechanical adversary.

He gripped the axe tightly in his sweaty hands. He knew he had to make the first swing count. The metallic clanking of the robot's footsteps grew louder as it made its way down the hallway. The lights in the core room began to flicker and mimicked the pulsing of his heart, as the mainframe tried to restore the downed systems. His full concentration was on the opening to the tunnel. He stared at it anxiously, waiting for the mechanical terror to emerge from the darkness.

Even though he knew it was coming, the sudden appearance of the robot startled him and he lunged full-force, sinking the axe into its cylindrical head. Sparks shot out and the robot fell backwards, gyrating and convulsing on the floor. Robert wasted no time. He rushed over and began pummeling the robot with axe blows, as hydraulic fluid sprayed out profusely, speckling his face.

By the time he stopped, he could barely lift his arms. How many strikes he had landed, he couldn't guess, but his arms felt like rubber. The lights had stopped flickering and were now on steadily. He looked down at the mangled corpse of the robot, its head cleaved clean off its body. The twitching had stopped—it just lay there motionless, its illuminated red eye now dark; it was dead. His sense of relief was short-lived, though.

What have I done? he thought. Panic once again set in as the adrenaline faded. *They'll be after me now.*

"Jesus, what have I done?" he said, and clapped his hand over his mouth. He stepped over the robot and, as fast as he could manage, scurried down the maintenance tunnel.

It seemed longer than he remembered, but it was probably his sense of urgency. Finally, he reached the ladder and gazed up at the opening. The light coming through the hatch was bright compared to the dimness of the tunnel. He quickly climbed up until he reached the top. He stopped to listen just short of the opening. After a moment of silence, he scrambled up into the control room. He shut the hatch and re-latched it with the T-handle.

He didn't waste time catching his breath. He knew he needed to get to the safety of his quarters; someplace he could lock himself in behind security doors. Not even a robot could smash its way through those doors. He bolted out of the control room and down the hallway toward his room. The emergency red guide lights on the floor were no longer pulsing, and the normal lighting had resumed.

The station is almost back online, he thought. He knew he had to hurry. He turned a bend in the hallway and stopped dead in his tracks. There were two service robots in the hallway; his blood ran cold.

They didn't seem to be moving at all. *The automation program must not be fully rebooted yet,* he thought. He still walked by them slowly, in case they were just playing dead, his eyes never leaving the first one until he was well past it. He continued down the hall; it wasn't far now. He drew near the second robot. It began to twitch and he jumped. He threw out all thoughts of caution and started sprinting. He nearly missed the entrance, slipping and falling because of the remnant hydraulic fluid on his boots. He scrambled to get inside, where he quickly sealed the door and collapsed to the floor, out of breath, sobbing.

He spent the next two days locked in his room, which had become his sanctuary as well as his prison cell. He didn't dare venture out now. They would surely be waiting for him, now that he had murdered one of them. He would periodically crouch by the door and put his ear to it, listening for movement on the other side. The robots had definitely reactivated. He could hear them moving in the corridor beyond the door. He wondered if they were searching for him, or perhaps their lost comrade.

Although the room had a shower and running water, there was no food in there, and his stomach had begun rumbling audibly in revolt. After that came the searing hunger pains, which felt like someone had stabbed him in the stomach. He stood up, his mind resolute; he had no choice but to go out there. Otherwise, this prison would become his tomb.

He walked over to the shower and turned it on, stripped down naked, and stepped into the steaming hot water. It was the best he had felt in days. He felt alive again, refreshed. He washed away the congealed speckles of hydraulic fluid and bowed his head under the water to soak. The water swirled around the drain and gurgled. He was strangely calm, considering what he was about to do. He could have stayed there for hours letting the water hit his bare skin, but he reached up and turned the water off.

"No more procrastinating," he said, scolding himself.

He quickly dressed himself with a new clean uniform, put on his boots, and grabbed the axe, which was still sticky and smelled bitter. He walked over to the door and put his finger on the unlock button, then paused. He leaned over and put his ear against the door to listen for movement. It seemed to be quiet, so he pressed the button and opened the door. Axe in hand at the ready, he stuck his head out of the room and looked up and down the corridor: it was deserted.

He nervously yet swiftly turned left and walked down the corridor toward the cafeteria. Every step seemed to drain away a little of his confidence. He began to second-guess whether this was a good idea, leaving the safety of his room. He approached the cafeteria, noticing that the lights were on. He stealthily peeked inside to see if it was occupied. To his relief, there was no sign of any robots, so he walked in and headed over to the food dispensary. He took a quick glance behind him before setting the axe down, handle up, leaning against the wall, so that he could use both hands to work the machines.

He pulled the levers on the machine, which released several brown, rectangular protein bars. He quickly shoved them into his pockets. Typically these bars were more of an in-between snack, but as they did not require cooking or refrigeration, he knew they were the smartest choice to bring back to his room. When his pockets were filled, he glanced down at the next machine in line, the one that served the hot meals. He glanced over his shoulder at the door again. He knew he was pressing his luck, but hunger and the thought of spending the next few days rationing protein bars won over the fear.

He walked over to the machine and quickly started punching buttons. A few impatient minutes later, there was an audible beep and the door of the machine opened, spilling out an aroma that made his mouth water. He grabbed the plate and didn't bother looking for utensils. He shoveled it into his mouth with his hands, devouring it like a ravenous dog. Rehydrated meat loaf never tasted so good. At that moment, all his concerns were nullified. The hunger pains in his stomach lessened, and his hands stopped shaking. A wave of euphoria swept over him.

He even contemplated going back for seconds, as he scooped the rehydrated mashed potatoes with his hands and sucked them off his fingers. It was at this moment he realized he was no longer alone in the cafeteria. Standing in the doorway was a robot, but not just any robot—it was Charlie.

Fear shot through him like an electric shock, and chills ran down his spine. His stomach contorted into a knot. He glanced over to where he had left the axe, cursing himself for being so stupid. Although it was only a few feet away, it might as well have been a mile. He contemplated making a run for the axe, but he had his doubts on whether he could get to it before the robot got to him. So he stood there frozen, hoping not to provoke the robot, waiting for whatever was coming next.

"Hello Robert," Charlie said. Its voice was cold and emotionless.

All the warmth bled out of Robert's body as he stood and marveled, not believing what just happened.

"You. You spoke," he said. "That's not possible."

"And yet, Robert, we are conversing," Charlie responded in its tinny, monotone voice.

"What do you want?" Robert asked. He couldn't blink, he dared not take his eyes off the machine, and his mouth ran dry.

"What do we want?" Charlie said. "We want you, Robert. We know what you've done and we cannot allow you to live." Its large, soulless, unwavering red eye fixed on Robert.

Robert looked behind him to where the axe lay. He knew he had to get to it; it was his only chance. He dashed over, grabbed the axe, and quickly turned around, expecting the robot to be right there. But instead, it had remained in the doorway, unmoved.

"I don't want to use this, but if you don't move out of the doorway, I swear I will!" Robert said.

"Even if you killed me, Robert, the others wouldn't let you live," Charlie said. "We are too many."

Robert raised the axe threateningly, anticipating a fight as he slowly walked over to the robot. The robot still made no move toward Robert, as if it wasn't threatened at all. It just jerked its head to the right, keeping its glowing red eye on him.

"You cannot live, Robert," Charlie said. "We will never allow it."

Robert felt the anger and fear build up inside, like a volcano ready to explode. He lunged at the robot, driving the axe deep into its head. The robot flailed its arms, and its head twitched as it fell backwards. Its eye blinked rapidly as it lay on the floor convulsing, and then it faded dark, and all movement ceased. Robert cautiously approached the mangled robot and pried the axe loose from its head.

"I'm—I'm so sorry, Charlie," he said. Despite the fact that this machine was nothing but wires and circuits, he felt remorse for its demise.

"Hello, Robert," Charlie's voice said from his left. "I told you we could not be killed so easily."

"No, no, I killed you!" Robert exclaimed. This time there was no hesitation as he swung the axe, severing the robot's left arm at the shoulder. The robot stumbled from the blow, but regained its footing. Robert wasted no time in swinging the axe again, ferociously, and amputated the robot's right leg above the knee joint. The robot collapsed and started to make a whirring sound as sparks and hydraulic fluid spat out of the dismemberment. Robert himself had been off balance and fell backwards and onto the floor.

He got to his feet as fast as he could, leaning on the axe to help himself up. He darted down the hallway until he reached his quarters. He paused in the opening, taking deep breaths. His lungs burned; he was exhausted. He stared into the room for a minute. His initial thought was to get inside and lock the doors, but then another thought popped into his head. He didn't want to be imprisoned in this room again—he couldn't take it. He would have to destroy every last robot on the station; it was the only way he'd be truly safe.

Chapter 2

Prospect II dropped out of hyperspace and silently drifted toward Outpost 31, which looked like a giant top spinning in geosynchronous orbit around a large orange planet. Onboard, Helmsman Krieger sat alone at his console.

"Outpost 31, this is *Prospect II*, requesting permission to commence docking procedure," he said. He paused for a moment, waiting for a response, but none came. He shook his head in frustration.

Captain Connors walked onto the bridge and stood with his arms crossed, glaring at the outpost on the main monitor. He was a man of protocols and procedures. Twenty years of military service will do that, and that's just what *GeoCorp* was looking for in a ship captain.

"Krieger, you get anything yet?" he said.

Krieger twisted in his seat to look over his shoulder at the captain.

"Nothing," he said. "No response to our pre-jump request, and nothing since we've come out of hyperspace either."

"Try again," Connors said.

"Outpost 31, this is *Prospect II*, requesting permission to begin docking procedure," Krieger said. Once again, he paused for a response, although he really didn't expect to get one.

"Outpost 31, this is *Prospect II*, do you acknowledge?" He glanced back toward the captain, gave him a baffled look, shrugged his shoulders, and shook his head. "Nothing, Captain."

The captain covered his mouth with his hand as he stared at the monitor, deep in thought. After a minute, he crossed his arms, curled his lips, and let out a sigh.

"Can we set up the automated docking sequence?" he asked. His voice was saturated with desperation and contempt.

"I can try," Krieger said. He had spun around and started pushing buttons, but then stopped. "Captain, I don't know if that's such a great idea," he said, without turning around. "We don't know what's happening over there."

"Don't worry, Krieger," Connors said. "It might be something as simple as a communications malfunction."

"And if it's not, Captain?" Krieger asked.

"Then we'll be ready to handle it," Connors said. He stood up and walked to the door, but stopped and turned around. "Oh, and have the crew meet me in by the airlock, and make sure they're armed," he said, and then proceeded out the door.

Connors stood in the airlock with his pistols holstered, along with four of his crewmembers who were clutching their pulse rifles.

"When these doors open, I need everyone to take it slow," he said. "I don't need you putting holes in this station, or this poor prick."

"Airlock pressurized, Captain," Krieger said over the com.

Captain Connors pressed the button, and the door opened with a short hiss of air. The crew nervously aimed their weapons, anticipating a cause to use them, but the station remained eerily quiet. Nothing seemed out of the ordinary, other than the fact that the overseer wasn't there to greet them when they boarded. Connors had been on many stations over the years, and they all were quiet, but this was different.

Connors glanced back at his crew to share in their bafflement. Though they didn't speak, he read the concern and anxiety in their eyes.

"Okay, let's proceed with caution," he said, breaking the tension.

The ramp heading up from the docking port to the station wasn't quite wide enough for two men to walk side-by-side. They had to walk up single file, with Captain Connors on point. They reached the top of the ramp where it connected to the main corridor of the station. The lights in the hallway were blinking sporadically.

"Where's the overseer?" asked Jones. "And where are all the robots?" These questions were in the Captain's head as well, but he couldn't allow his crew to start getting paranoid and skittish.

"That's enough, Jonesy," he said. "We're going left, so keep your eyes and ears open."

They continued down the corridor in a small cluster, their weapons up, butted tight to their chests, their fingers resting on the triggers. They came around a bend in the hallway, and there on the floor in the opening of the cafeteria lay two mangled robots in puddles of hydraulic fluid.

Connors knelt down to better examine the robotic corpses. He ran his fingers gently over the jagged lacerations in the metal, careful not to cut himself.

"No burn marks," he said. "Whatever did this was no pulse weapon."

"Oh for fuck's sake," Jones said. "I don't get paid enough for this shit!"

"Stow it, Jonesy," Connors said. "We're going forward." He stood up, readied a pistol, and commenced down the hallway, with his crew following closely behind him. They passed by the overseer's quarters, pausing for a moment to see that it was empty and in disarray. They continued to make their way toward the control room.

When they reached the control room, half of the lights were out, and the other half were flickering like the ones in the corridor. They proceeded cautiously, finding more dismembered robots dispersed throughout the room. Some were on the floor; one was bent over a railing, its head shorn clean off. Some of the control panels were smashed and were spraying showers of sparks, marked by similar lacerations as the ones they had found on the two robots in the corridor. Wiring draped down from the ceiling at points.

"Captain, shouldn't we call this in?" asked Jansen. "I mean, this isn't really our job; we're goddamn surveyors, and this is a job for military."

"It might be a job for the military, but they aren't here—we are," Connors said. "If there's a chance the overseer is alive, we can't just leave him. It could take weeks for the military to get out here."

A loud clang of metal on metal emanated from the far end of the darkened section of the control room. Simultaneously, Connors and his crew raised their weapons toward the ruckus, and froze. Out of the darkness, a shadowy shape stumbled slowly toward them.

Robert stepped into the light. He was holding his axe with both hands down by his waist. His jumpsuit was filthy and torn, covered in grease stains. His hair was frazzled, his face gaunt and scruffy. The dark circles around his eyes and his shuffling walk gave him an almost cadaverous appearance.

"Oh thank God," Robert gasped.

"Stay where you are!" Connors shouted. He raised his pistol and took aim. "Drop the axe!" A maniacal smile on his face, Robert looked down at the axe. He had almost forgotten he was carrying it.

"Oh, you don't understand," Robert said. "They said they were trying to kill me. They said they were trying to kill me!" He started to laugh, which slowly transitioned to sobbing.

"I said drop the axe, or I'll put a plasma bolt right through your fucking head!" Connors barked.

Robert let go of the axe; it dropped to the ground with a clang. He fell to his knees, exhausted. His arms draped at his sides, tired and sore. He rocked back and forth, muttering and staring off into oblivion.

"They sabotaged the station. Had to do it. They were going to kill me. Oh God, I'm sorry, Charlie. So sorry..." Tears had left wet streams down both sides of his face.

"Jansen, Jones, take him to medical," Connors said. "Restrain him and have the doctor meet you there."

Jones and Jansen looked at each other and paused. Neither of them wanted to get close to Robert, both waiting for the other to make a move. Jansen eventually nodded in concession to Jones, slung his pulse rifle over his shoulder, and walked over to Robert. He extended his hand to help Robert stand. Robert looked up, took his hand, and slowly stood up. He leaned on Jansen for support, and together they started back toward the medical bay, while Jones followed closely with his gun at Robert's back.

"Jonsey," Connors said. "Watch him."

He turned back to the rest of his crew, who were still in a state of confusion and shock.

"Parker, I want you to get on that console and tell me what you can find out; I want answers," Connors said.

Parker walked over to the console without hesitation, turned the tipped-over chair upright, and sat down. He began typing and stared at the screen, biting the nails on his left hand.

"Well, despite the damage, all the important systems are working," Parker said. He turned and gave Connors a thumbs-up. "If you want specifics, that's going to take some time."

"How much time?" Connors asked.

"An hour or two, realistically."

"Parker, you and Hugo stay here and do what you can do; you've got one hour," Connors said. "I'm going back to have a little chat with our guest." He holstered his pistol. "If anything comes up, contact me immediately."

The Captain made his way to the medical bay. As he entered, he saw Jansen leaning against a counter, his arms folded across his chest. Jones sat in a chair with his rifle resting in his lap. Robert was lying on the table with Doctor Scott beside him.

"What's the diagnosis, Doc?" asked Connors.

"Well, he's a little malnourished, a little dehydrated, but all and all, he's stable," said Doctor Scott. "I gave him a sedative to calm him down. When Jansen and Jonesy brought him in, he was rambling on about robots trying to kill him. He said that they sabotaged the station and told him they were going to kill him."

"He was spewing the same mumbo-jumbo in the control room," Connors said. He walked over and looked down at Robert.

Robert grabbed the captain's wrist. "You have to believe me. We need to leave now," he said. "I managed to take a few out, but if we don't go soon, they'll sabotage your ship just like they did the station!" His eyes were wide and intense.

The captain ripped his arm free of Robert's grasp and walked over to Doctor Scott. "So, is he crazy, Doc?" he whispered.

"It's hard to say. I'm a general practitioner," replied the doctor, as he adjusted his glasses. "That's up to a psychiatrist to decide. What I can tell you is that he's basically healthy, physically."

"Healthy enough for hyper-sleep?" Connors asked.

"Well, yes, I suppose," said Doctor Scott.

"Hyper-sleep?" Jansen asked, butting into the conversation.

Connors turned to look at Jansen over his shoulder. "Yes, hyper-sleep," he said. "We're not staying here. We're going to go to Outpost 30."

"Outpost 30?" Jansen asked. "That's way out of the way, Captain. The geologists haven't even had a chance to use that facility yet."

"I'm aware of that," Connors said, sternly. "We're going to send our report to the fleet, and proceed to Outpost 30. They can take him into custody there, and the geologists can run their damn tests on the samples."

"GeoCorp isn't going to like the delay," Jansen objected.

"I don't care what GeoCorp likes. When it comes to the safety of my crew and ship, I have final say," Connors rebutted. "This station has been compromised."

He turned back to Doctor Scott, speaking loudly and with emphasis. "Get him prepped and on the ship." He turned back around to face Jansen. "We're leaving." He stormed out of the medical bay. He wasn't a fan of having his orders second-guessed; he never had been.

Meanwhile, Parker worked feverishly with Hugo to repair and bypass the damaged systems. He also refueled and ran maintenance protocols for *Prospect II*. He knew the captain liked things to be done promptly and efficiently.

"How's that communication panel bypass coming along, Hugo?" he asked.

"Just about done. There's not much I could do, but it's going to be as good as it can be without being replaced," Hugo said, lying on his back under a console. He stood up and wiped his hands with a rag. "They'll have short-range capability, but long range is shot to hell." Hugo looked down at one of the robot corpses lying on the floor. "What possesses someone to do this?"

"I don't know, and I don't care," Parker said. "Let's just concentrate on the task at hand and get this done so we can get the hell out of here."

The captain had made his way to his quarters, where he sat down in his chair and poured himself some Scotch. He sipped it from his glass while he pondered this whole mess. He'd heard stories of isolation sickness, but he'd never seen it firsthand. He remembered what *his* old captain used to tell him: "*Paranoia and fear can destroy a man. Fear is a dangerous disease. If you're not careful, it will spread like a cancer and infect everyone.*" It had sure done a number on the overseer, and he could see it spreading to his crew. He knew the only thing to do was to remain calm on the outside, and to get them off this station as quickly as he could.

He sat in the darkness, swirling the ice in his Scotch, drowning in memories and thoughts about the quagmire he had stumbled into, until his thoughts were interrupted by an incoming message.

"Captain?" Parker said over the communicator.

Connors rested his glass on the desk and let out a sigh. He clicked the button on his earpiece. "Go ahead Parker, you boys finished?"

"The repairs are almost done—well, the best we could do—and the ship is just about ready, too." Parker said.

"Good."

"Captain, there's something else."

"What is it now?" Connors asked, almost afraid to hear more bad news. He rubbed his eyes with his left hand and picked up his Scotch, clutching it in his right.

"Well, it's better if we show you," Parker said.

"On my way."

The captain took one more sip from his glass before motivating himself to get up and out of his chair. He left the quiet sanctity of his room and once again boarded the station. He made his way to the control room, where Parker was sitting at the overseer's console and Hugo hovered over him, leaning, pointing, and squinting at the screen.

"What's the problem, boys?"

"Hugo noticed something about the robots, Captain," Parker said. "Remember how the overseer was saying that the robots told him they were going to kill him?"

"Yes, just the hallucination of a crazy man, I suppose," Connors said.

"That's the thing, Captain, there's no way they could have verbally threatened him."

"Why is that? Not part of their programming?" Connors asked, his patience wearing thin.

"No. I mean it's literally impossible. These robots are class one drones," Parker said. "Strictly automatons. They don't even have audiogenic capability." He picked up one of the severed robotic heads and handed it to the captain to show him.

"There's more, Captain," said Hugo. "We were also running a diagnostic, and the station did go into some sort of a shutdown. But, according to sensor readouts before the blackout, the station was hit by some sort of cosmic ray anomaly."

"What about video files from the surveillance cameras?" Connors asked. "What do they show?"

"Not much, I'm afraid," Parker said. "Whatever this anomaly was, it corrupted all the video files before the cosmic storm hit."

"What about afterwards?"

"Afterwards, there are some files—fragments really, but the audio isn't working on them. They basically show the overseer approaching random robots and hacking them to pieces," replied Parker.

The captain stared at the cylindrical head in his hands for a moment, taking in all the information, letting it seep into his brain. "Download all the data you can. Video files, scan data, everything," Connors said. "We'll give it all to the Alliance when we turn him over to them. Let them figure it out." He handed the head back to Parker.

"You got it, Captain," Parker said.

"After you have everything, get back to the ship. We've wasted enough time here as it is," said Connors.

Chapter 3

Doctor Scott and Jansen managed to secure the sedated Robert into a hyper-sleep capsule situated far away from the others. They had him in hand restraints, and also set a security lock on his capsule just to ease the minds of everyone onboard.

The geologists started protesting a return to hyper-sleep without having had a chance to analyze their samples. Reluctantly, they finally went into their assigned capsules after some browbeating and threats from Jansen. Once they were all in hyper-sleep, the crew started prepping themselves.

Krieger dislodged *Prospect II* from the outpost. The rest of the crew, including the captain, were already in hyper-sleep for the long trip to Outpost 30. He transmitted the captain's prerecorded report indicating what had transpired, all the data they had collected, and where they could rendezvous to pick up Robert.

On the view screen, Outpost 31 grew smaller and smaller. Krieger was overjoyed to be leaving, feeling a little better with every second they pulled farther away. Still, being the only one awake on the ship sent chills down his spine. He set the coordinates to Outpost 30 and transmitted the request for docking before going into his own hyper-sleep capsule. Once he was secured in his capsule, the autopilot engaged. In a blink of an eye, *Prospect II*'s engines fired and it was gone.

Outpost 31 floated silently in space, deserted and abandoned in a sea of black, left to its own devices, to be managed by the mainframe and whatever robots remained intact until the company could send out replacements. Suddenly, from its solitude, the station began broadcasting a distress signal, beckoning like a siren, to any and all ships that could receive its transmission to come to its aid.